The Magic Cube #3

I0582596

The Quest for the Crown

By Mitchel Maree
Illustrations by Ola Snimshchikova

Text Copyright © 2022 by Mitchel Maree
Illustration Copyright © 2022 Ola Snimshchikova

First paperback edition February 2022
Hardback edition: February 2022
ISBN 978-1-7360656-3-1 (paperback)
ISBN: 979-8-8309494-9-1 (hardback)
www.mitchelmaree.com

Dedicated to my amazing nieces and nephews
Mylee, Andrada, Drew, Sydnie, Everett, D.J., Averi, and Kinley.

The more that you read the more things you will know. The more that you learn, the more places you'll go! -Dr. Seuss

Other books in the Magic Cube Series:

Contents

Chapter One

Vacation

"I can see the beach," six-year-old Parker Watson announced from the back seat of the car. She turned her body and pressed her face as close to the window as possible, the seatbelt cutting into her shoulder.

The Watson family was traveling to a vacation rental by the sea. For the next week, they would spend their time playing on the sand, splashing in the water, and searching for seashells.

Max, Sophie, and Violet turned to take in

the view. Clear blue water sparkled in the distance. Waves danced across the surface, building slowly before folding over to crash into the shore, leaving a trail of white foam behind.

"I can't wait to go to the beach," Parker said, squirming in her seat. She could almost feel the soft sand squishing between her bare toes.

"I wonder how cold the water is?" Violet asked softly.

"I don't care," Max, the oldest, replied. "I'll go swimming no matter what."

"Are you coming in with us, Dad?" Sophie asked, bouncing up and down in her seat.

"Someone has to toss you into the waves," Dad teased, pulling the car into a short driveway.

"What about you, Mom? Are you coming

in the water this time?" Sophie pressed the button to release her seatbelt.

"Mom doesn't swim." Violet reminded her older sister as she climbed out of the car.

Mom shrugged. "I like to keep my toes in the sand. Besides, someone has to help build those magnificent sandcastles." She gave her kids a wink.

"Can we go to the beach now?" Parker asked, struggling to untangle herself from the seatbelt.

"Let's get settled first." Mom laughed. "Take your bags and go find your rooms. I've got to get this food into the fridge."

"Find your swim gear, too," Dad said, unlocking the front door. "Bedrooms are up the stairs."

Max, Sophie, Violet, and Parker grabbed their bags from the trunk, rushed into the house, and hurried up the stairs.

There were three bedrooms in the house. One room had a bunk bed and a single bed; the other two had one double bed in each. The girls took the room with three beds, while Max took the room directly across the hall from his younger sisters.

"I'm taking the bed." Sophie tossed her bag on top of the single bed. Being the oldest girl had its advantages, she always got to pick first.

"I'm sleeping on the bottom bunk," Violet said.

"That's not fair," Parker protested with a foot stomp. "I don't even get to choose. Being the youngest stinks."

"Girls! Come check out this backyard," Max called from across the hall.

Sophie, Violet, and Parker rushed into the bedroom, joining their brother at the window.

"Looks like a mess," Parker said, wrinkling her nose as she peered outside.

The yard was overgrown and looked uncared for. A rusty lawnmower sat lost amidst the tall grass. What appeared to be an overturned wheelbarrow stuck out of a bush covered with thorns. A few bare trees scattered the landscape.

"What are we looking at exactly?" Sophie asked.

"There's so much to explore out there," Max replied. "Look at all those huge tree-like bushes in the middle of the yard. It might be bamboo; maybe we can hollow out the middle and make a cool fort."

"Race ya!" Parker pushed past her older siblings, excited to check it out.

"Careful on the stairs," Sophie called, flinching as Parker ran down them at full speed.

"We're going out back!" Max yelled toward the kitchen, not waiting for an answer.

Sliding past Parker, he burst through the back door. In one giant leap, he jumped from the porch, gliding over the set of stairs leading down into the yard.

Copying his movements, Parker also jumped from the porch, paying no attention to the distance from the ground. She landed hard, losing her balance, and tumbled onto her knees. Brushing off her pants quickly, she scrambled up and raced after her brother.

Violet and Sophie were more cautious, choosing to walk down the four stairs into the yard.

The children waded through patches of yellow dandelions and tall grass, heading toward the tightly packed bamboo in the center of the yard.

Max gently pushed aside some of the stalks, discovering the space within had already been cleared out.

"This is amazing!" He looked around the open space. "This should be our official hideout for the week."

"Our own secret society," Sophie declared, spreading out her arms.

"Maybe we can have a campout," Parker added.

"I don't know about that," Violet protested, shivering. "Creepy crawlies come out at night. I don't want to wake up to spider webs in my hair."

Parker rolled her eyes. "You're no fun."

"Hey, what's that?" Sophie asked suddenly. "Something moved in the corner over there."

"What? Where?" Parker whipped her head around. "I don't see anything."

"It was a flash of pink," Sophie said, then shook her head. "Maybe I'm just seeing things."

"No, you're not. Look!" Violet pointed to another spot.

In between the bamboo stalks sat a stuffed pink and purple unicorn.

"How did it get over here?" Violet walked toward the toy. Before she could reach it, the unicorn disappeared. "Where did it go?"

Violet bent down to examine the spot where the unicorn had just been. Instead of a stuffed toy, a familiar cube sat between two stalks.

"The magic cube!" Violet held it up in her palm. The cube had buttons on the top, a lever on one side, and switches on another side.

Max reached out to take the cube from her. Before he could snatch it, Parker grabbed the cube from Violet, quickly pulling the lever and pushing the various buttons and switches.

"Hey, that's my job!" Max glared, crossing his arms over his chest.

The last two times they found the magic cube, Max had been the one to press all the buttons. Parker gave him a smug look.

Like before, a sudden burst of blinding light flashed across the sky, followed by complete darkness. Seconds later, the sun was shining again as if nothing had happened. The siblings all looked at each other expectantly.

"Now what?" Sophie asked.

"The branches are moving!" Violet yelled, pointing toward the opposite side of the fort.

The children turned around. Jaws dropped as they watched the branches part before their eyes. A pathway, wide enough to walk through single file, had been created through the bamboo stalks. At the end of the path sat the pink unicorn.

Shoving her brother aside, Parker walked quickly toward the stuffed toy. As she stretched her hand out to grab it, the unicorn disappeared again.

"What the heck?" Parker looked around.

"Are we're still in the backyard?" Violet sounded disappointed.

"That's odd," Max said, glancing around at the tall bamboo still surrounding them. "Usually, the magic cube transports us *somewhere*."

"Pink!" Sophie pointed. "I see pink through these bamboo stalks."

"Let's investigate." Parker wiggled her

eyebrows. Quickly, Parker pushed through the tall bamboo, forcing her way out into the open. "Oh, my goodness! You guys have to see this!"

Chapter Two

Pink

Max, Sophie, and Violet exchanged looks before shoving their way through the bamboo.

"Everything is pink!" Violet exclaimed, eyes darting from one spot to another, trying to take it all in.

Swirling pink cotton covered the landscape before them. Instead of grass, strings of pink covered the ground. Trees, their branches covered in pink puffs, lined the border of the open field they stood in.

Bushes of thick spun sugar dotted the area.

A thick scent of pure sugar hung in the air.

"It looks like a cotton candy machine exploded," Max commented.

"Do you think it *is* cotton candy?" Parker licked her lips and picked a piece of the pink fluff from the ground.

Sophie sniffed the air a few times. "Smells like a carnival."

"Tastes like it, too." Parker's eyes widened as she licked the pink off her fingers.

"Ew, don't eat that." Sophie covered her mouth with her hand.

"I feel like we're in the board game, *Candyland.*" Violet scrunched up her face and walked through the field.

"I love that game." Parker scanned the ground. "I don't see the colored squares, though."

"There's a path over here," Max called, waving his sisters over.

The pathway was covered in tiny white pebbles. Parker stepped on the path, gravel crunched under her foot. Curious, she jumped down on all fours sniffing at the ground.

"What are you doing?" Sophie asked, her eyebrows scrunching together. "Get up."

Parker didn't listen. Instead, she picked up a piece of gravel and popped it in her mouth.

"Parker!" Sophie screamed. "That's disgusting! Don't eat that!"

"It's sugar!" Parker laughed, giving her sister a goofy grin.

"Sugar crystals?" Max made a face. "That's interesting."

"Try it." Parker grabbed a handful and

extended her palm toward her siblings.

"Eww," Sophie covered her mouth and shook her head back and forth quickly.

"I'll take your word for it," Max said, putting his hands up.

Violet took a small rock, twisting and turning it in her hand before placing it on her tongue. "Oh, that's good."

"Gross," Sophie muttered under her breath.

Parker shrugged and licked the remaining sugar off her fingers. "Your loss."

"Let's see where this path leads," Max said, getting everyone back on track.

The girls followed him, their footsteps crunching on the sugar crystals with each step.

As they walked, Parker extended her hand, grazing it lightly over the pink fluff next to her. The cotton stuck to her open palm. Parker licked her hand, tasting more of the sweetest cotton candy she had ever eaten.

"You guys have to try this." Parker stopped walking. "It's so good."

"I don't know." Sophie shook her head. "Doesn't seem very sanitary. Animals poop and pee in fields."

"I don't see any animals out here," Violet commented, taking a handful of pink fluff. "Oh, wow! I can't even explain how good this is. Melt in your mouth good."

Max nodded in agreement, his mouth full of spun sugar.

"You're going to get a stomachache if you keep eating everything you see," Sophie warned them.

Parker rolled her eyes. "We're just sampling. It's not like I'm gonna roll around in the field with my mouth open." Parker paused and lifted her eyes toward the sky, a smile creeping across her face. "Actually, that sounds fun."

"Fine," Sophie caved. "I'll try some, but I'm picking off a bush."

Sophie grabbed a handful of fluffy cotton from the nearest bush.

"Ouch," a voice cried out.

Immediately dropping the cotton candy, Sophie jumped back, a look of horror on her face. "Sorry. I'm sorry."

"Is that bush alive?" Parker whispered, not taking her eyes off the talking plant.

The bush rustled and shook. The three girls took a giant step backward while Max leaned in closer to investigate.

Two large, purple eyes blinked at Max.

"Eek!" he cried. "The bush has eyes!"

The bush shook more as something pink and

fuzzy pushed out of the branches.

"Oh, sorry about that," a pink unicorn said. Bits of pink fluff flew in all directions as the unicorn shook herself off. "Didn't mean to frighten you. I'm always getting caught in those bushes. The branches get tangled in my fur, and the cotton is so sticky."

The children stood, staring, their mouths hanging open. Of course, they shouldn't have been surprised by a talking unicorn. After all, the magic cube had taken them to the North Pole and through a fairy door.

"Well, that was not the entrance I was going for." The unicorn laughed. "I'm Samena. You must be the famous Watson siblings."

"We're famous?" Parker asked in awe.

"Oh, yeah," Samena said, her head bobbing up and down enthusiastically.

"Everyone is talking about you four. You helped capture Krystal. She was planning on stealing all the magic in Noradoon."

The children exchanged glances.

"Noradoon?" Max repeated, unsure.

"Yes," Samena replied. "That's our world."

"This place is called Noradoon?" Parker scrunched up her nose. "Doesn't seem to fit with the candy theme you got going on here."

"No, no." Samena laughed. "*This* is Frosted Falls. Our *world* is Noradoon."

The children continued looking around, still not quite understanding.

Samena shook her head and rolled her eyes. "Forget it. It's not important. What's important is the Sapphire Crown."

"Ohhh, that sounds pretty." Violet's eyes lit up.

"It is pretty." Samena agreed. Then her face fell. "But it's missing. Someone stole it, and we need to find it."

"Why would someone steal it?" Sophie asked.

"Because of its magic," Samena replied, a far-off look in her eyes. "The crown holds all the magic of Noradoon."

"What kind of magic?" Violet asked, curious.

Samena rocked from side to side. "All kinds of magic. Everyone in Noradoon uses some type of magic. But whoever holds the Sapphire Crown can control the magic. Not only that, but the crown can also open the portals between each of our lands."

The children stared at the unicorn blankly.

"We move between our lands by portals," Samena clarified. "You have to be invited into a land that is not your own. For instance, I can't go to the North Pole unless invited. If I had the Sapphire Crown, I would be able to go there whenever I wanted."

"Is that a bad thing?" Parker asked.

"It depends on your motive." Samena tilted her head toward Parker.

"What's a motive?" Parker asked, leaning closer to Samena.

"Your reason for doing something," Max answered.

"Exactly," Samena said. "Someone could move through each portal and steal magic, for one. Not to mention, the Sapphire Crown opens the portal into *your* world, too."

"Who would want to go into *our* world?" Violet asked, placing a hand on her chest.

"Someone looking to rule the humans,"

Samena said. "There are dangerous creatures in Noradoon; you do not want them running free in your world."

Violet felt a shiver run down her spine. "We better find that crown."

Samena began to pace. "The crown was stolen from Magic Meadows, the unicorn's land."

"Wait! Didn't you just say no one can go through a portal without being invited?" Max asked, rubbing his chin.

Violet gasped, slapping a hand over her mouth. "Are you saying a unicorn stole the crown?"

Chapter Three

The Gummy Forest

"Why would a unicorn steal the crown?" Sophie asked.

Samena shrugged, letting out a deep sigh. "We don't know, but we think the thief is hiding here."

"Why here?" Violet asked.

"Maybe they were hungry." Parker shrugged, looking around.

"The sweets are good," Samena agreed. "Frosted Falls is actually the only neutral place in Noradoon. Anyone from any land can come here without an invite. Plus, it's safe. Nothing dangerous lives here."

"Well, where do we start?" Max ran his hand across the tops of the pink bushes.

"We start by finding Dreckson." Samena furrowed her pink brows. "He's an all-knowing owl. Maybe he saw something unusual."

"An owl! Great idea," Violet said. "Where do we find him?"

Samena trotted down the sugar path. "The Gummy Forest."

The path led them past trees wrapped in pink clouds. As they neared the edge of the field, the landscape changed. Long strands of rubbery-looking green grass replaced the fields of pink cotton. Large colorful boulders took the place of fluffy pink bushes.

"Is this stuff edible?" Parker asked.

"Try it," Samena encouraged her.

Parker didn't hesitate. She pulled up one blade of the bright green grass and shoved it in her mouth.

"Licorice. Green apple," she said between bites.

"You're going to make yourself sick," Sophie warned her.

Parker sighed. "I'll try to control myself, but I might need a blindfold for this adventure."

"Oh! My! Goodness!" Violet rounded a corner and stared in front of her. "Parker, you definitely should cover your eyes for this."

Parker ran ahead, knowing she shouldn't look but unable to fight her curiosity. Her eyes widened as she took in the forest before them.

The thick tree trunks were made entirely

of chocolate. Branches burst out in all directions, covered with gummy bears, gumdrops, and gummy fruits in all shapes, sizes, and colors. Gummy Forest smelled like a freshly opened chocolate bar. Parker felt her tummy growl at the sights and smells surrounding her.

Samena jumped up and snapped a pretzel-looking branch off a tree. "Try some. Just don't—"

"Get greedy," Parker mumbled. "I know."

The children plucked juicy gummy bears off the branch and popped them into their mouths.

"So good," Max commented. "Can we eat this branch? It looks like a pretzel."

Samena shrugged. Max took a careful bite, moving it around in his mouth to test all the flavors.

"Salty," he said.

"I want to try some tree bark," Violet said.

Gently, she peeled a square of chocolate from the tree trunk and inhaled the sugary scent before taking a bite. Her eyes closed as the chocolate melted on her tongue, tasting sweeter than any chocolate she had ever tried.

Parker hurried over and pulled another piece free, shoving it in her mouth and swallowing with a loud gulp.

"Slow down, Parker," Max said. "Take your time. Enjoy all the flavors."

Parker rolled her eyes. "Trust me. I can enjoy it just as much by gulping it down."

Suddenly, there was a loud rustling in the branches above them. A few gummy bears fell from the limbs as the tree shook ever so slightly.

"Whoo! Whoo eats from my tree?" a voice called down to them.

"Is that an owl?" Sophie asked, searching the branches for the owner of the voice.

"Of course, I'm an owl," he answered rather abruptly, jumping down the branches to get closer to them.

"Now, *Whoo* are *you*, and *why* are you eating my tree?"

"Sorry, Mr. Owl, sir. Your tree looked yummy," Max said, looking sheepish.

"It's rather rude to eat other people's houses," the owl snapped.

"Want it back?" Parker opened her mouth to show off the half-chewed food inside.

"Parker!" Sophie shouted, grabbing Parker's arm and pulling her back. "That is not okay."

Parker snapped her mouth shut and glared at the owl.

"We're very sorry, sir," Sophie said as sweetly as possible. "We didn't realize this was your tree."

The branches shook more as the owl popped out from behind the gummy treats to stand on a limb directly above them. The owl stared down at them with two fried egg gummy eyes. His head and body were red and green, blending perfectly with the contents of the tree. His wings were covered with gumdrops; white sugar crystals sparkled across the tops. His legs looked like two fat gummy worms fanning out at the tips to form claws.

"Whoo are you?" the owl repeated through a candy corn beak.

"I am Samena." She gave a small curtsy as she spoke. "These are the famous

Watsons. You must be the distinguished Dreckson, the all-knowing owl."

"Ah, yes." Dreckson puffed out his green gummy chest. "The all-knowing *and* all-seeing."

"We're looking for the Sapphire Crown," Samena continued. "It was stolen. We believe the thief is hiding somewhere in Frosted Falls."

"The unicorns lost the Sapphire Crown?" Dreckson pulled a wing to his beak dramatically. "How irresponsible."

"It was stolen," Sophie reminded the owl.

"Oh, how exciting!" Dreckson fanned out his wings, hopping from foot to foot. He craned his head toward Samena. "A traitor among the unicorns? Oh my!"

"Yes, it's all *soo* fascinating." The words dripped with sarcasm as Samena tried to hide her irritation. "Have you seen anyone suspicious run through?"

"Besides you?" Dreckson said arrogantly. "I can't say I have. Nothing out of the usual. Unless you count a bunch of ragamuffins eating from my tree."

"I can eat your wing if you'd prefer," Parker snapped, taking a step toward the owl.

Dreckson gasped, pulling a wing towards his chest. "I have no time for this. The unicorns should learn to keep their valuables locked up more tightly."

"It was stolen," Sophie said harshly.

"I haven't seen it." Dreckson turned his head away from them. "Now go away. Leave me and my tree alone."

Violet threw her hands in front of her in frustration. "I thought you were all-seeing and all-knowing?"

"I am," Dreckson snapped, turning his

head back around his body. "I only see what is important. So-called unicorns and greedy humans are of little significance to me."

"The crown is important to every single creature in Noradoon," Samena reminded him. "You know if the crown falls into the wrong hands, all the portals will be left unprotected. That includes Frosted Falls."

"Imagine all the little human children running free in your forest." Parker licked her lips and rubbed her palms together. "So many yummy treats."

"Greedy hands touching everything." Max wiggled his fingers for effect.

"I'd give this place a day." Sophie looked around.

Dreckson shivered, narrowing his eyes. "I haven't seen the crown. Perhaps the gnomes can help you."

"Where can we find the gnomes?" Sophie

asked.

Dreckson glared down at Samena. "A unicorn should know gnomes live in Lollipop Fields." Waving a wing in dismissal, he said, "Now leave my forest."

Chapter Four

Lollipop Fields

"Lollipop Fields?" Parker groaned. "Why can't it be something I don't like?"

"You like everything!" Sophie laughed.

"I don't like broccoli," Parker sneered. "Broccoli fields would be better than lollipops."

"The owl pointed this way." Max continued down the path.

The trail wound through Gummy Forest, passing endless rows of gummy-filled trees. Parker put her hands next to each eye, using them as blinders to block out all the delicious treats surrounding her.

They walked through a final row of trees and into another open field, this one covered in tall rainbow-swirled lollipops.

"There must be a million lollipops," Violet said in fascination.

"It smells like *The Sweet Shop* back home," Sophie said.

Parker stuck out her tongue and licked the air.

"What are you doing?" Max looked at Parker like she was crazy.

"I wanted to see if the air tasted like candy." Parker shrugged. "It kind of does."

"You're so weird." Sophie shook her head.

"Where do you think we'll find a gnome?" Max looked around. "What does a gnome even look like?"

The field contained endless rows of lollipops. The lollipops came in all shapes, sizes, and colors, similar to a field of wildflowers. There were large and small circles, heart-shaped ones, cone-shaped ones, and long spiral ones, all with rainbow swirls.

Violet tapped a finger on her lips. "Gnomes are typically small. I think they live underground, so we should start down at their level."

The others watched as Violet dropped down to her hands and knees and took off, crawling through the lollipop stalks. The children looked at one another, unsure whether they should follow or not.

"I found something!" Violet popped up near the middle of the field, waving wildly.

"The gnome?" Max called, weaving his way through the lollipops.

Violet pointed down toward her feet. "A patch of mushrooms."

Everyone dropped down to their knees. A patch of red and white swirled mushrooms covered a small area hidden beneath the towering lollipops.

"Mushrooms?" Samena scrunched her nose.

"Finally, something I don't want to eat," Parker groaned.

"Gnomes live in mushrooms," Violet informed them. "This has to be a gnome village."

"If you say so." Sophie shrugged.

If anyone knew about gnomes, it was Violet; she always had her nose stuck in some fairy-tale book.

"It doesn't look like anyone lives here," Samena said, looking around the small clearing. "It's so quiet."

"Well, they live underground," Violet explained. "The mushrooms are more of an entry point, not a house."

"How do we get there?" Parker asked, confused. "Are we going to shrink down again?"

Parker remembered their last adventure when they had shrunk to the size of fairies, wings and all.

Violet shrugged. "I don't know. Let's see if we can find a doorbell or secret lever somewhere."

"Maybe we just push down on the mushrooms," Max suggested, gently pressing down on the top of one.

Surprisingly, a small chime of bells echoed inside the mushroom.

Parker impatiently reached out and pressed down on the mushroom repeatedly.

"All right, all right. Enough already," a

small voice came from inside the mushroom.

A creak sounded as a door opened from one side of the mushroom. Out popped a tiny gnome, looking similar to the statue sitting in the garden back home. She wore a red shirt and purple overalls; a matching purple hat sat on her head.

"Oh, company." She straightened her back and brushed off her overalls. Clearing her throat, she said, "Greetings. I am Sidonia of the family Rayburn. You may call me Sidray."

"Pleasure to meet you, Sidray." Violet gave a curtsy. "I am Violet of the family, Watson. These are my siblings, Max, Sophie, and Parker. And Samena of the unicorns."

Max covered his mouth to hide a chuckle.

Sidray gave a bow in return. "How may I be of assistance?"

"The unicorns need your help," Samena answered.

"Oh, helping animals is sort of my thing!" Sidray leaned back against the mushroom. "We gnomes take care of animals and nature."

"The Sapphire Crown is missing," Samena said.

Sidray let out a gasp and stood upright.

"It was stolen," Parker whispered, leaning in as if it were a big secret. "There's a thief on the loose here."

"A thief! The crown stolen!" Sidray jumped back and clutched her chest. "This is horrible news."

"Have you seen or heard anything out of the ordinary? Hooves running overhead or something?" Samena asked, hopeful.

"Well, unicorns are always running around these fields," Sidray said with a shrug. "You know how much unicorns love it here."

"Did you hear any hooves recently?" Samena tried again.

"No," Sidray shook her head. "You should know all the great hiding spots considering how much unicorns love playing hide n' seek."

Samena looked down. "I don't get to play much."

"How about these fields?" Max suggested.

"Oh, no. There are far too many gnomes scattered through Lollipop fields," Sidray told them, tapping her chin thoughtfully. "I would probably hide in the Chocolate Mountains."

"Not chocolate," Parker groaned. "That's my favorite."

"The Chocolate Mountains are huge,"

Samena groaned. "Any hints on where to start?"

"I think you would know better than me," Sidray laughed. "Unicorns are always playing in and around the mountains. Especially since you can fly there; it's so dangerous crossing the—"

Before she could finish, a loud scream filled the air. It sounded like the high-pitched shriek of a toddler throwing a temper tantrum.

The children looked at one another with wide eyes.

The unicorn froze.

Sidray rolled her eyes, crossed her arms over her chest, and stamped one foot impatiently.

"Dragons?" Max's eyes darted back and forth across the sky. "Please don't let it be dragons again."

"Dragons would be better." Sidray sounded annoyed. "That's the banshee."

"The what and the who, now?" Max whipped his head toward the gnome.

"The banshee." Sidray gave another eyeroll. "She *loves* to scream and screech and wail for hours on end. It's enough to give anyone a pounding headache."

The screaming rang through the fields again. The children covered their ears with their hands, which did little to block the noise.

"It's getting closer," Samena whispered, backing into a thick patch of lollipops. "I'd hide if I were you."

Sophie looked frightened. "What happens if she sees us?"

"Stick some cotton in your ears because it's going to get loud," Sidray said, unamused.

"Louder than she already is?" Parker yelled over the noise.

"Maybe once she sees us, she'll quiet down," Violet said hopefully.

"The banshee never quiets down." Sidray sighed.

"She's right," Samena called from her hiding place. "Hide while you still can."

The screeching intensified as the banshee flew directly over their heads.

"Too late," Samena whispered. "Whatever happens, I was never here."

"Me neither!" Sidray quickly rushed back into her mushroom and slammed the door.

The children looked up. A ghostly creature fluttered directly over their heads, its red eyes staring down at them.

Chapter Five

A Ghostly Creature

"It's a ghost," Parker said.

"Creepy," Sophie whispered out one side of her mouth.

The banshee hovered above them, her long, dark hair flowing behind her. Her pale skin was almost blinding against her dark dress. Red eyes continued to bore into the children. Slowly, she opened her mouth to let out another scream.

Max pressed his palms tighter against his ears. "I wish she would stop doing that."

The banshee floated down, hovering just above the ground. The children kept their eyes on her, not sure what to do. The banshee looked at them for a moment before releasing a low wail.

Violet felt a great sadness flow through her entire body. Her eyes filled with tears as the banshee continued to cry.

"What's the matter?" Violet asked, taking a step toward the creature.

"She's putting a spell on you," Samena whispered harshly from her hiding place.

Violet glanced over her shoulder to where the unicorn hid. "No! Her pain is real. I can feel it."

"No, it isn't," Samena argued. "She's a ghost; ghosts don't have feelings."

"I feel sad too," Parker sniffed. Quickly, she brought her hands to her ears. "Stop it. Go away, ghost! I don't wanna cry."

"She's pulling you into her eternal sorrow," Samena warned them. "Cover your ears, or you may never be happy again."

"Samena is probably right." Sophie gently laid a hand on Violet's arm. "What if it *is* a spell and you spend the rest of your life feeling sad?"

"You're both wrong," Violet said roughly, jerking her arm away from Sophie. "Look at her. She's really sad."

"That's how they get you," Parker warned her sister, hands still pressed to her ears.

The wailing stopped as the banshee watched Violet slowly approaching her. She floated just above the ground, swaying lightly as if in a breeze.

"Violet." Max reached toward his sister.

Violet shook her head and held up her

hand. Max let his arm drop. "Be careful."

"The banshee has her under a spell now," Samena said, poking her nose between two lollipop sticks. "Might as well leave them to stare at each other."

The banshee suddenly turned toward Samena and screamed loudly. Samena scrambled back, startled by the outburst.

Violet carefully reached out a hand, placing it on the banshee's arm. When she felt cold flesh, her eyes swung quickly up to meet the banshee's gaze. How was she touching a ghost?

"I'm not going to hurt you," Violet said softly. "We want to help. It hurts when you scream, though. I can't hear what you're trying to say."

"Are you trying to reason with a banshee?" Samena laughed from somewhere in the bushes.

The banshee stayed silent, looking at Violet.

"Maybe you can help us." Violet tried again. "We're looking for the Sapphire Crown. It was stolen, and we think the thief might be hiding here."

The banshee let out a low moan, followed by a quiet whimper. Slowly, she lifted her arm and pointed to a spot across the fields. Without another sound, she floated up into the air and took off in that direction.

"I think she knows where the crown is," Violet said excitedly.

"We should follow her," Max agreed.

"Adventure!" Parker yelled, taking off through the field.

Sidray popped her head out of the mushroom. "Good luck."

"This seems like a bad idea." Samena crawled from her hiding spot, shaking herself off.

"That's my line," said Sophie, glaring playfully at Samena.

"Don't forget about--" Sidray's warning was interrupted by another loud screech from the banshee.

"What did you say?" Sophie turned, but the gnome was gone.

Shrugging, Sophie ran to catch up with her siblings, who were already halfway through Lollipop Fields.

They weaved through the fields, twisting and turning in and around the lollipop sticks. Finally, they burst out of the fields and into a large open meadow. The ground before them was covered in thick mud; small patches of yellowed grass grew haphazardly throughout the area.

"Looks like a marsh," Max said, looking down at his feet.

"Look, in the distance." Sophie pointed. "Those have to be the Chocolate Mountains."

A shriek rang out across the marsh. The banshee circled the air, where dark brown peaks sliced into the sky.

Max took a tentative step onto the muddy surface, testing to make sure it was solid. Carefully, he took two quick steps before stopping on the first patch of grass.

"I think it's safe," he called. "Move slowly. Try to get to these grassy patches. They're solid."

Max moved forward, leaving a deep imprint with each step. The mud became thicker and stickier with each step. As they moved across the marsh, each step sunk down deeper and deeper.

"Hold on." Max suddenly held up a hand; his foot had sunk up to the ankle. "I just lost my shoe."

"I can't move my foot!" Parker called out, struggling to pull her foot out of the sticky mud.

Max looked down to find both his feet had sunk under the mud, and the ground was rising. The grassy patches disappeared below the surface.

"Well, this isn't good," Max mumbled.

"I'm sinking!" Parker yelled, trying to pull her legs from the mud. "I can't get my legs out!"

Max moved quickly toward Parker, reaching out a hand to pull her free. "You girls keep moving. Don't slow down. Just run!"

"We need to go back," Sophie protested.

"We're halfway across," Violet pointed out.

"We don't have time to stand here

discussing it," Max said harshly. "If we keep moving, we won't sink."

Max yanked on Parker's hand. With a sucking sound, her legs pulled free from the muck.

"Move!" Max gave Parker a gentle shove.

"I can't walk in this." Parker felt her feet sink down deeper with every step.

"We have to keep moving," Max told her. "I'm right behind you."

The children moved as fast as the sticky mud allowed. Every step was an effort as they sank down to the ankle and then yanked their feet free.

"This is going to take all day," Sophie whined.

As they neared the edge of the marsh, the ground began to move around them. A small ripple gently passed next to them.

Then another.

And another.

"What is that?" Sophie's voice trembled.

Little by little, the ripples grew bigger and wider.

"We're almost there." Max tried to hide the urgency in his voice. "Keep moving. Try to pick up the pace a little."

"Something smells really good!" Parker sniffed the air.

"How can you think about food right now?" Sophie asked roughly.

"There's no time. Keep moving!" Max ordered.

The mud began moving like a current.

"It's getting easier to move," Violet said.

"I think the mud is turning into a river of some sort," Sophie agreed, feeling slightly relieved.

"Or an ocean," Parker yelled, pointing behind them.

The mud behind them moved swiftly, pulling back to create waves. Waves slowly began to rise into the air, crashing down mere inches from where they stood.

Chapter Six

A Sticky Situation

Mud splashed into the air as the waves crashed down. Sticky goo flew into their face and hair.

"We've got to get out of here!" Samena came hopping across the top of the muck. "Taffy Marsh has a mind of its own. I told you that banshee was up to no good. She's trying to kill us!"

"Taffy?" Parker looked around. "That explains why it's so sticky and smells so good."

"We're almost at the shore," Max called. "Hurry, those waves are getting bigger."

As if on cue, a large wave grew behind them, splashing down and pushing giant glops of taffy toward them. Parker lost her balance and face planted into the goop.

"I got you!" Max cried, grabbing the back of Parker's shirt and pulling her upright. "We gotta move. NOW!"

"We're going as fast as we can!" Sophie yelled back. "Telling us to move every second isn't helping!"

The taffy pushed and pulled as they struggled to reach the shore.

"I can't move! I can't move!" Violet screamed, desperately pulling at her legs. "I'm stuck!"

"Keep going!" Max ordered, waving his other sisters on. "Don't stop until you reach the bank. We'll be right behind you!"

Max reached for Violet's hand as another big wave crashed behind them, burying them up to their waists.

"Max, what do we do?" Violet's eyes filled with fear.

"I can't move." Max tried to hide the fear in his own eyes. "The more I struggle, the more I sink."

"But if we don't move, we'll be buried in taffy," Violet said quietly.

Suddenly, another massive wave grew behind them, splashing down and pushing them forward through the muck.

"It's moving us." Max sighed with relief.

"What if a wave crashes on top of us?" Violet asked.

"Let's hope that doesn't hap...." Max stopped mid-sentence, his eyes following something rising behind Violet.

Max and Violet felt themselves being

pulled backward as a colossal wave arched up behind them. Max kicked his feet violently, but he was stuck, helpless to move away from the wave towering over them.

When the wave crashed down, Max knew it would bury them. He wondered if he could somehow push Violet to safety.

Violet turned to see what Max was staring at. Max grabbed her face before she could look. Slowly, he shook his head. It was better if she didn't know.

"I'm scared." Violet trembled.

Max grabbed his sister's hand. "It's going to be all right. Whatever happens, don't let go of my hand."

The wave continued to swell behind Violet. Max braced for impact.

The banshee's shriek filled the air, high-pitched and deafening. Max looked up and saw her flying over the wave. In an instant, she flew down, wrapping her arms around Max's waist and yanking him up out of the taffy.

"Don't let go!" Max yelled to Violet, gripping her hand as tightly as he could. "Grab my wrist with your other hand."

Violet did as she was told, grasping Max's wrist as tightly as possible.

"Go, go, go!" Max shouted at the banshee.

Violet struggled to break free. Kicking her feet as fast as possible, she glanced over her shoulder and spotted the enormous wave towering over their heads.

Finally, one foot pulled free, and she continued to kick the other frantically.

"Good job, Violet," Max yelled. "You've almost got it. Hurry!"

"I'm trying." Violet gritted her teeth as

her heart hammered in her chest.

With a loud slurping sound, the taffy released its hold on Violet's foot. As if on a slingshot, Violet, Max, and the banshee were sent flying backward through the air. The banshee soared, shrieking and wailing as she struggled to regain her balance while keeping her hold on Max.

The banshee fell silent as she regained control and headed toward the mountains. Max and Violet turned to watch the giant wave crash down violently on the spot they had just vacated.

"That was close," Max whispered.

"Too close." Violet was still shaking.

"There's Sophie, Parker, and Samena!" Max pointed down to where his sisters were still struggling to get free of the taffy, inches from the bank.

The banshee let out a soft screech, one

that didn't hurt their ears. Quickly, she flew over a small river, depositing Max and Violet on the other side. Without stopping, the banshee flipped around and headed back over toward the marsh. Reaching down, she grabbed Parker's arm, yanking her free and setting her on Samena's back. Then, she grabbed Sophie and pulled her from the sticky goo.

Max and Violet watched as Samena spread her wings and began flapping wildly, trying to free her hooves from the taffy. The banshee, still holding Sophie, pushed with her free hand until Samena was up and out of the muck.

"Phew! That was scary," Violet commented.

Sophie and the Banshee landed next to them, covered from head to toe in taffy goop.

A large splash came from the river, followed by a scream, one that didn't belong to the banshee.

"Parker!" Sophie yelled. "She's in the river. She can't swim!"

"I'm coming!" Max called out. Without hesitation, he ran to the river's edge and dove into the dark waters. "Stop fighting, Parker. Kick your feet and reach for my hand."

Parker bobbed up and down in the water. Despite her struggle, her head dipped beneath the surface. She resurfaced, coughing and sputtering, thrashing her arms desperately.

"Grab my hand!" Max reached out for her.

Max had never seen Parker look so scared; she was always so fearless. Parker went under again. This time, she didn't pop back up.

"Parker!" Max dove under the surface, searching the murky water for his sister. Their hands grazed as he reached out for her, but the current pulled her away.

Max resurfaced, struggling to catch his breath. He turned toward the shore, yelling, "Do you see her? I can't see her!"

"There!" Sophie pointed.

The banshee sprang into action, soaring into the air and splashing down into the water. She dove under the surface, passing Max as she swam.

"Where did she go?" Max looked around him.

Suddenly, the banshee burst through the water, shooting up into the sky like a geyser. Water rained down on Max as the banshee flew over his head. A small figure lay limply in her arms.

Gently, the banshee laid a lifeless-looking Parker onto the ground in front of Sophie and Violet.

"Parker?" Sophie's voice trembled as she kneeled beside her sister. "I don't think she's breathing."

Violet dropped to her knees, pushing as hard as she dared on Parker's stomach. Water shot from Parker's mouth as she sat up, coughing and sputtering.

"Tastes like root beer," she said between coughs.

Max laughed as relief rushed through him. "I think she'll be all right."

"You smell like root beer." Violet gave her sister a sniff.

"That is Root Beer River after all," Samena commented.

"Hey, I was a root beer float," Parker said with a grin.

Her siblings all laughed in relief; Parker was just fine.

Chapter Seven

A Startling Discovery

"I smell chocolate." Parker pushed herself up into a sitting position.

"Look behind you," said Violet.

Parker's eyes grew wider and wider as she turned and saw an endless row of chocolate-covered mountains. The tops were covered in rainbow sprinkles. Small strings of white frosting ran down the sides.

"This is torture." Parker licked her lips.

Max climbed out of the water. He looked down at his clothes and shoes. "I'm so sticky. I wonder if this stuff will ever come off."

Sophie nodded. "It will be interesting explaining this one to Mom and Dad."

"What is that?" Violet peered through a gap in the mountain range.

The children followed her gaze. The land beyond the Chocolate Mountains appeared to be on fire. Red and orange rock formations covered the entire landscape. Smoke rose from cracks along the ground, covering everything in a haze.

"That is the border of Vatrena Dolena," Samena said with a shiver.

"Va-train what?" Parker asked.

"Va-tren-a Doe-lean-a," Samena pronounced slowly. "The Valley of Fire."

"The land of the dragons?" Violet remembered the name from their time with the fairies.

"Yes," Samena took a step back. "Stay far away from there."

"Unicorns don't like dragons?" Max made a mental note.

"Nobody likes dragons," Samena said.

"I met some dragons; they weren't horrible," Max told her.

"They were nice," Violet agreed.

Samena gave them a sideways glance. "Sure, baby dragons are nice. Then, they grow up and learn to hunt. Not so nice anymore."

"Do dragons eat unicorns?" Violet scrunched up her face.

"Probably," Samena shrugged. "I'm not getting close enough to find out."

"There are so many caves in these mountains." Sophie looked through several different openings. "Where do we start?"

The scream of the banshee filled the air.

Samena rolled her eyes and let out a deep sigh. "Here we go again."

"Give her a chance," Violet said. "She's been helpful so far."

"Really?" Samena asked sharply. "First, she tried to hypnotize you into eternal sadness. Then, she tried to drown us in Taffy Marsh. That isn't what I'd call helpful."

"She saved us from Taffy Marsh." Violet reminded her. "She saved Parker from drowning, and she led us here."

"I don't trust her." Samena turned her nose to the air.

"Let's see what she wants." Max made the final decision.

The children headed toward the banshee. Samena kept her distance, staying a few feet behind them, not hiding her distrust.

"She wants us to go in here." Violet

peered past the banshee into a dark cave.

"We could get lost in there," Sophie said.

"We have the banshee." Parker completely trusted the ghostly creature. "She'll keep us safe. Let's go check it out."

"I have a bad feeling about this," Samena said, dragging her hooves.

Inside, the cave was large and open, but the light didn't reach the dark corners.

"See." Samena felt triumphant. "It's just an empty cave."

"Wait! Something's twinkling over there." Violet walked to one corner, reaching out a hand. "It's a crown!"

Parker rushed forward, stopping short when she came face-to-face with a set of wide, purple eyes. Parker jumped back in surprise as a unicorn identical to Samena stepped out from the shadows, blocking the crown.

"Samena has a twin!" Parker yelled.

"She's not a unicorn." The second unicorn shook her head. *"That's an imposter."*

"Don't be ridiculous." Samena laughed. "You're a liar and a thief. Now give me the crown."

"I'm not giving you anything," the unicorn said. "You're the thief. You stole the crown; I took it back from *you."*

"Then why are you hiding?" Max questioned, a look of doubt crossing his face.

"I'm hiding from *her,"* the unicorn insisted. "I couldn't make it to Magic Meadows. She would have stopped me and taken the crown."

"Give me the crown, imposter!" Samena ordered impatiently.

"I'm not the imposter!" the unicorn

insisted.

"Stop!" Violet demanded; her brow furrowed in thought.

"The banshee! She's in on this!" Samena protested, pointing toward the ghost girl. "She has you questioning everything!"

The banshee let out a shriek. Violet narrowed her eyes, watching the interaction between the banshee and this second unicorn.

"Samena might be right, Violet," Sophie said.

"Why would the banshee lead us to the crown if she was helping a thief?" Max scratched his head.

Violet turned toward the imposter. "Why haven't you used the crown yet?"

"I don't want to *use* the crown. I want to return it to my mother," the unicorn said. "Besides, you can't use the crown without the scepter. Something your thief over there forgot to grab."

"This is ridiculous." Samena stamped her hooves. "Give me the crown so *I* can return it."

"You didn't know about the scepter, did you?" The unicorn taunted. "Otherwise, you would have brought it with you."

Samena glared at the unicorn, blowing air out her nostrils. "You are really getting on my nerves."

Violet turned toward Samena, surprised by the change in her tone. The light, airy voice was now deep and almost dark sounding.

"Why are you so angry?" Violet asked Samena.

Without responding, Samena charged at the imposter, knocking her to the ground. Samena grabbed the crown and hurried out of the cave.

The banshee shrieked, throwing herself at Samena, struggling to hold her down.

"Get off me, ghost!" Samena roared.

The banshee held on to Samena, screaming as loudly as she could. Max took a step forward to break up the scuffle. He stopped in his tracks when Samena suddenly roared back at the banshee. The roar sounded as if a startled lion had wandered into the cave.

Samena shoved the banshee off her and flew into the air. Black smoke swirled around her, casting a dark shadow over her bright pink fur. Shocked, the children watched as Samena's coat turned black, darker than the midnight sky. Her eyes glowed an eerie golden yellow. Her horn disappeared, and a thick black mane tumbled down her back.

The banshee shrank back into the shadows of the cave, whimpering.

Samena let out a whinny loud and low. "Thank you for your help. That stupid banshee would never have led me here without you."

With a cruel laugh, Samena grabbed the crown in her teeth and flew out of the cave.

"Stop her!" the other unicorn called. "Don't let her escape!"

It was too late. Samena was already outside the cave entrance. Quickly, she turned and kicked the mountainside several times with her powerful hooves.

"Bye-bye," she teased before flying away.

Rocks and debris began falling from the walls inside the cave.

"It's caving in. We have to get out of here!" Max called.

A large boulder fell from the ceiling,

landing directly in front of the entryway, trapping them inside the collapsing cave.

Chapter Eight

A Unicorn Princess

The unicorn bent her head down, her horn glowing. A flash of light burst from the tip, slicing the giant boulder in half, creating a pathway they could escape through.

"You're definitely not the imposter," Parker said, impressed.

"We have to go, now!" Max ordered, leading the way out of the cave.

As soon as they were all safely outside the cave, Violet asked, "What just happened?"

Rocks continued rolling from the top of the mountain behind them. Another huge boulder fell, blocking the entryway once again.

"There isn't much time to explain," the unicorn told them. "I'm Averly, daughter of Empress Emree, the ruler of Magic Meadows, the land of the unicorns. That other creature is a pooka."

"A what?" Sophie interrupted.

"A pooka," Max repeated. "Shapeshifters. I read all about them in my Irish mythology book. Their normal shape is a dark horse, but they can shift into other creatures."

"Shapeshifting. That must be how Samena got through the unicorn portal," Violet said.

"Yes," Averly said urgently. "And it's how she'll get back in. She'll go back for the scepter now; the crown won't work without it."

More rocks rolled down the mountainside, stopping at Parker's feet. Her eyes darted around quickly before she reached down and popped the stone into her mouth.

"Gross!" Sophie stuck out in her tongue in disgust.

"It's delicious," Parker grinned.

"We have to get to Magic Meadows," Averly said. Glancing at the crumbling mountains behind her, she quickly muttered, "Oh, I should fix that first."

Lightning flashed from her horn; several bolts shot out at once this time. The rumbling and crumbling of the Chocolate Mountains stopped.

"We can't have those falling," Averly sighed.

"The dragons could get in," Parker

pointed out.

"Oh, the dragons." Averly flicked her tail absently. "They're mostly harmless, and they don't like sugar. Now, we need to get out of here. Banshee, can you help me carry these children toward Frosted Falls?"

"I thought we *were* in Frosted Falls." Violet looked confused.

"I mean *the* Frosted Falls." Averly gave a wink. "Max and Violet climb on my back. Banshee, can you carry the other two girls?"

"How do you know our names?" Parker looked at her suspiciously.

"Everyone knows who you are." Averly smiled. "Now, let's go."

Max helped Violet onto the unicorn's back, climbing up behind her. The banshee wrapped an arm around Sophie and Parker, following Averly into the air. They flew over Root Beer River, Taffy Marsh, and across Lollipop Fields, continuing until they came to a giant waterfall.

The waterfall streamed down a large rock canyon. Light sparkled around the waterfall as it cascaded down the rocks. The water splashed down into a bright blue pool, creating a churning white foam that looked like buttercream frosting.

Averly and the banshee landed gently along the soft, sandy bank leading into the water.

"This is Frosted Falls," Averly announced.

"It's beautiful!" Violet sighed.

"I'm tempted to dive in." Max tried rubbing his sticky hands together.

"Please do," Averly said. "This is the most refreshing water you'll ever swim in. Plus, it will wash off that sticky taffy in no time."

Max looked down. Strings of taffy hung off his shirt, making it look tattered and torn. Without hesitation, he waded in.

The water was the perfect temperature, cool but not freezing. Max dove all the way under the surface. When he popped back up, the taffy clinging to his clothes had vanished.

"I'm clean," Max called to his sisters. "Come on in; it's not deep; I'm touching the ground."

"I'm a sticky mess." Sophie scrunched up her nose as she touched her head. "My hair is crunchy. Eww!"

"My arms keep sticking to my shirt." Parker laughed.

Sophie and Violet slowly waded into the water. Parker took a running start before leaping into the air.

"Cannonball!"

She splashed into the pond sending a spray of water raining down on her sisters, earning a glare from Sophie.

"Follow me." Averly glided toward the waterfall.

"Where are we going?" Sophie asked.

"Magic Meadows." Averly winked as she ducked under the waterfall.

Violet's eyes widened as she followed the unicorn through the waterfall.

Averly was standing on a small beach, urging them forward. "Hurry. Samena is already there. I can feel it."

Sophie climbed out of the water and onto the beach, shocked when her clothes were immediately dry.

Averly led them through a narrow canyon. Parker pushed in front of everyone, not wanting to be left behind. She stopped in front of a solid rock wall draped in long green vines.

"It must be through here," Parker said. She pushed the vines to the side and scowled when the solid rock didn't budge. "There's nothing here. It's a dead end."

"That's because you're not a unicorn," Averly stated calmly. Squeezing past Parker, she used her hooves to push a series of random rocks. "Now try."

Parker moved the vines again. This time, light streamed through the canyon, revealing a doorway.

"Oh. My. Goodness," Violet breathed as she stepped through.

They stood on a hill overlooking Magic Meadows. Below them, unicorns jumped and splashed through flowing rivers and waterfalls surrounded by lush green fields. Sunlight danced across each body of water. The entire valley sparkled.

In the distance, a gray cloud stood out among the glittering valley.

"Looks like a storm is brewing," Max commented.

"That's no storm." Averly's body tensed. "That's the pooka. She's already made it to the palace. She's going after the scepter. We need to get down there. I need to be there when the battle begins."

A screech filled the air, sounding like a battle cry.

"You should warn a person before you do that!" Sophie glared at the banshee, a hand over her chest. "You just about gave me a heart attack. I could have fallen off this cliff."

The banshee stared at Sophie, blinking rapidly.

"You came through the portal too?" Parker asked, a look of disbelief on her face.

"Of course," Averly said with a shrug. Turning to the banshee, she asked, "Can you help me get everyone down to the palace?"

The banshee nodded and grabbed Parker and Sophie around the waist.

Averly flew toward the palace, landing nearby in a patch of trees. A thick, dark cloud enveloped the entire castle.

"What's the plan?" Max whispered, sliding off the unicorn's back.

"Stay quiet and follow me." Averly tiptoed on her hooves.

"No screaming," Parker hissed at the banshee.

The banshee frowned at Parker, letting out a low grunt.

One by one, they flattened themselves against the side of the palace, shuffling quietly toward the sound of voices.

"Where is the scepter, Empress?" Samena growled.

"We both know I can't tell you that," a gentle voice replied.

"You'll tell me, or I'll rip your castle apart piece by piece!" Samena shot back.

Max peered cautiously around the corner. Samena stood tall in the middle of the cobblestone courtyard. The empress was hidden in shadows.

"I'm willing to make a trade." Samena tried to sound sweet. "This crown for the scepter."

The empress laughed. "You really think I'll fall for that. One doesn't work without the other. You need both."

"Give it to me!" Samena's eyes flashed as she lifted into the air. "Or say goodbye to your precious palace!"

Dark clouds swirled around Samena,

electricity lighting the sky around her. Samena tossed her head back, laughing, as a lightning bolt shot straight toward the empress.

Chapter Nine

An Epic Battle

The banshee let out a piercing cry, louder and higher in pitch than before. She continued screaming as she shot across the sky, colliding in midair with Samena.

"Get off me, creature!" Samena yelled, shoving her away.

Dark clouds began encircling the banshee. She screamed in three short bursts followed by three long cries, over and over.

The children covered their ears, feeling as if their eardrums would burst at any moment.

"It hurts!" Sophie cried out. "What is she doing?"

"Calling for help!" Averly yelled back. "You four stay here. I'm going after that crown."

Averly burst into the air, weaving in and out of the dark clouds. The banshee flew back toward Samena, kicking her as hard as she could. The crown flew out of Samena's grasp.

"You'll pay for that!" Samena roared.

Red bolts of lightning flashed across the sky. Samena reached out and grabbed the banshee, shoving her into the path of a lightning bolt. Averly reached out, managing to grasp the banshee's arm, pulling her out of harm's way just in time.

Samena took that moment to kick Averly square in the stomach, sending both the unicorn and the banshee flying backward.

Parker, unable to stand by helplessly, ran toward the courtyard.

"Parker! Get back here!" Sophie yelled.

Max grunted and shoved off the wall, charging after his little sister.

Parker reached the courtyard just as the Sapphire Crown bounced on the cobblestone in front of her. Parker bent down and snatched up the crown. As delicate as the crown looked and felt, it had not broken.

"Are you crazy?" Max yelled breathlessly.

Before she could respond, a glittering blue unicorn stepped from the shadows. "I believe that's mine," she said softly.

Parker silently held the crown out for the empress.

"If you wouldn't mind." The empress

dipped her head, allowing Parker to place the crown on top. "Now, I would step back if I were you."

Immediately, her horn lit up like fireworks on the Fourth of July, spewing out colorful sparks in red, green, blue, and purple. Max pulled a frozen Parker back into the shadows.

"No!" Samena screamed as the colorful lightning bolts broke through the dark clouds.

The ground shook violently as the pooka landed like a bomb on all four hooves. Streaks of red light flashed from her eyes, like lasers, aimed directly at the empress. Lightning bolts pelted the ground, sizzling with each hit. Samena's hair flew wildly all around her as a powerful wind funneled over her head.

"Oh, she looks mad!" Parker said.

"Get back!" Max warned, pulling them further back toward the palace.

"We should help them," Violet said, rushing toward Max and Parker.

"It's too dangerous!" Sophie shouted, grabbing her arm.

"We can't leave them out there exposed." Violet pulled from her grip.

"What can we do?" Sophie asked.

Violet stepped toward the courtyard just as the sky filled with a bright light. Freezing in place, she looked up to see the light bursting from Averly's horn, smashing through the funnel cloud, breaking it apart. Back in the courtyard, a rainbow shot from the empress's horn, momentarily covering the dark clouds above in a colorful light show.

"Ok, I should probably stay here." Violet ducked back behind the building.

"Is that all you've got?" Samena taunted. "It's going to take a lot more than that to stop me."

"Like an army, perhaps?" Averly said, landing next to the empress.

"You two?" Samena laughed. "Not much of an army."

"I'll fight you!" Parker rushed from her hiding place.

Samena threw her head back in laughter. "What magic do you have?"

Max reached out and pulled Parker back. "You really are crazy. I think Averly was referring to *that* army."

The castle doors burst open. Unicorns poured out of the building, surrounding their empress.

"Is this a big enough army for you?" Averly teased.

Samena glared at the unicorns, her eyes

blazing red.

"Prepare for battle!" The empress shouted to the army behind her.

Every unicorn bowed its head. White light sparkled from their horns.

"Whoa!" Parker said. "I guess they got this!"

Samena continued to laugh. Sparks of red and blue electricity ran down her mane and tail, sparking off the tips.

Sophie reached up; her hair was standing on end. "That's a lot of electricity."

Samena pressed her front hooves together. A small blue ball appeared, growing larger as she pulled her feet apart. The blue ball sparked and spun in the air, popping and fizzing as it grew.

"That's a ball of pure electricity," Max muttered, pulling Parker behind him.

"Open the portal!" The empress yelled.

"Why would she open the portal at a time like this?" Max's question was answered when another piercing shriek filled the sky above them. This screech was louder and more intense than the banshee's cry.

Fire danced across the sky.

Max's head snapped up. "Dragons!"

Samena whipped her head around as an army of dragons broke through the storm clouds. Quickly, she threw the ball of electricity toward them, flying up into the air as fireballs poured from the sky.

The dragons flew in perfect formation, fire blazing from their open mouths.

"Surrender, Pooka," a booming voice bellowed from the front lines. "Or prepare to be vaporized."

Samena ignored the warning, continuing to pelt electrically charged bolts toward the dragons. She weaved around the fireballs, zigzagging across the sky.

"Attack!" the empress yelled from the ground.

The sky lit up in an array of colors. Bright, glittering sparks burst from the unicorn's horns. Red and orange fireballs, blazing from the dragons. Blue lightning bolts shooting across the sky. A brilliant flash of light filled the sky when all the elements slammed into each other. The light was so bright the children had to look away. If it hadn't been so terrifying, the sky might have been stunning.

A blast of colorful sparks wrapped around Samena. Kicking and screaming in the air, she broke free, sending another round of lightning bolts down toward the unicorns.

Using their horns, the unicorns created a shield. The lightning bolt slammed into the shield, immediately turning into pink fluff and falling harmlessly to the ground.

"You can't win this battle," the empress called to Samena. "Surrender. You've lost."

Samena's eyes flashed as she glared down at the empress. Sparks continued to fly off every inch of her body.

Behind her, three dragons broke formation. The first dragon rammed into Samena's side. Samena flew sideways, losing her center of gravity, and landing in the arms of a waiting dragon.

"Get your talons off me!" Samena shoved against the powerful dragon.

The dragon released his hold on Samena as the two other dragons circled around her several times.

"What the-," Samena snapped her head up as the electricity left her body. Suddenly, she felt herself falling from the sky.

Chapter Ten

Legends and Secrets

Glitter flew from the empress's horn, gathering into a soft pillow and catching Samena in mid-air.

"What did you do to me?" Samena demanded, her body wrapped in shimmery chains.

"Suppression chains," the Empress replied. "They make your powers useless."

"You may have captured *me*, but I promise you, I am *not* alone." Samena spat out the words. "An army is building, and they are coming for your crown. No one can stop us. Not you or your unicorns. Not those fire-breathing monsters. Not four useless humans. No one!"

"Who is leading this army you speak of?" the empress asked, stepping toward Samena.

"I think you already know." Samena laughed again, glancing sideways toward the dragons.

"Take her away." The empress waved a hoof.

Two dragons flew down, grabbing Samena and pulling her back up to the sky. The dragons retreated back toward their home.

"Once the dragons have left, seal the portal," the empress ordered, turning back to the unicorns. "Secure the area. Make sure no one is here who doesn't belong."

"Yes, Your Majesty."

In a cloud of dust, the unicorns thundered past them, heading toward the valley.

"That was loud," Parker coughed, swatting the dust away from her face.

"What was all that about?" Averly asked her mother. "An army? Who's coming for us?"

"There are many myths and legends in Noradoon, dear," the empress said gently. "Many stories created simply to cause fear and panic. Don't let a pooka get to you."

"Why did she look at the dragons?" Averly pressed. "I thought they were our protectors."

"They are, Dear." The empress shook her mane. "That is why pookas fear them. Now, I'm being rude and must greet our guests." The empress turned toward the children.

"I'm Empress Emree, ruler of Magic Meadows. You are the famous Watson children."

"Why does everyone keep saying we're famous?" Parker scrunched up her nose.

"You are," Empress Emree said. "The magic cube has chosen you four as the human protectors of Noradoon."

"I still don't know exactly what Noradoon is," Sophie commented.

"I have something that may help," Empress Emree told them, lifting a hoof and moving it in a circle.

A rolled-up scroll appeared in front of her.

"Take this." She nodded toward the scroll.

Max reached out and pulled the paper toward him. Carefully, he unrolled the thick parchment. "A map?"

"That is Noradoon," Empress Emree said.

Max laid the map gently on the ground. The paper crinkled as he worked to smooth the edges down with his hands.

"Look! It's Emerald Valley." Sophie pointed to a forested area near the edge of the map. "That's where the fairies live. We've been there."

"There's the North Pole!" Parker pointed. "We went there too."

"And now we've been here." Violet pointed to Frosted Falls.

"So, we live on Earth." Sophie began to understand. "You live in Noradoon."

"Yes." Empress Emree nodded. "Two worlds, side by side. Connected by a portal that can only be opened by three things. The magic cube. The Sapphire Crown. Santa's hat, but that one only works on Christmas Eve."

"You said the magic cube chose us," Max said thoughtfully. "Why?"

"We don't know." Empress Emree shrugged. "The cube brings help to Noradoon when we need it most."

"We're just kids," Parker said.

"We don't understand the magic of the cube," Empress Emree confessed. "It feels a power within you four. Look at all you have done for Noradoon so far. Kids or not, you've saved Christmas, the fairies, and now the unicorns."

"Is something bad coming?" Max felt a shiver run down his spine as if sensing something terrible. "We can help with small things, but a war?"

"Don't let the pooka scare you." Empress Emree smiled. "Talk of war and legends is simply a fear tactic. A way to scare us all. It means nothing."

A cold breeze blew through the trees.

"We should go home," Max said quickly, rolling up the map and shoving it in his back pocket.

"Thank you for returning the crown," Empress Emree said. "Averly, show them the way home."

"Yes, Mother." Averly nodded.

"I'm flying on the unicorn's back this time," Sophie said quickly.

Averly shook her head. "No need. I know a shortcut."

The children followed Averly into the trees. She ducked down, crawling on her belly into a thick bush. The children copied her movements, wiggling like worms.

When they came out the other side, they were back in the pink fields where their adventure had begun.

"This is where we first met Samena,"

Violet said.

"She must have just come through the portal," Averly shook her head.

"I can't believe she tricked us," Sophie said.

"There are many secrets and creatures in Noradoon," Averly said. "I was the one who sent for you, not Samena. I bet she was scared when she first saw you."

"She did seem surprised." Violet tapped her chin. "But she recovered quickly."

"She must have realized you could help her," Averly said. "Then, simply kept pretending to be a unicorn, knowing you would lead her to the crown."

"What's the deal with the banshee?" Parker asked.

"The banshee is another mystery of Noradoon," Averly said. "She showed up long ago. The leaders of the lands granted her free passage between all the portals of Noradoon."

"Why?" Violet asked.

"We aren't sure." Averly shrugged. "A legend lost over time."

"There's the magic cube!" Max raced forward and grabbed it.

"And here is where I say goodbye," Averly told them.

"Say goodbye to the banshee for us," said Violet.

"I will," Averly promised, disappearing back into the pink bush.

"Ready?" Max pressed the buttons and pulled the lever on the cube.

They walked through a row of cotton candy sticks, arriving back inside the bamboo fort.

"That was a yummy adventure." Parker licked her lips. "But, I'm still hungry."

"Max! Sophie!"

"Dad's calling us." Sophie scrambled out from the bamboo.

"There you are," Dad said. "Ready to go to the beach?"

"Yes!" Parker scurried past Dad into the house.

"Did you find some cool hiding places out there?" Dad asked as Max bounded past him.

"Super cool," Max replied.

"Hey, Max," Dad called.

Max turned in the doorway.

"You don't want to lose this." Dad winked as he tossed the magic cube up the stairs to Max.

The End

NORADOON

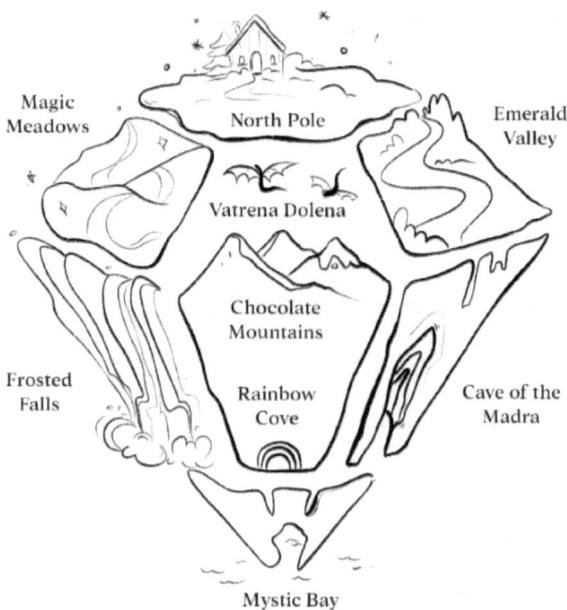

Author's Note

Ireland is full of myths, legends, and folklore. I loved learning about the Pooka (Púca) and the Banshee (Bean-Sidhe).

The pooka is a shapeshifter who usually takes the form of a dark horse; but can be seen as a dog, rabbit, or even a man. While the Pooka isn't dangerous, they are known for creating mischief and exaggerating the truth, finding it hilarious to trick humans.

The Banshee is a female spirit who wails and cries a warning of pending death. The ghost does not cause death but instead warns of death so families can prepare.

Some believe the Banshee is the spirit of a descendant who died long ago, arriving to guide a family member to the other side.

In this story, the Banshee protects the unicorns and the Watson children. She is not a messenger of death; however, she does have a deep connection to the Watson family, which will reveal itself later in the series.

I hope you enjoyed the story.

I love writing the Magic Cube Adventures and would love the opportunity to share these books with readers everywhere. As an author, reviews are the best way to show others how much you enjoyed a book. If you liked this book, it would be fantastic if you gave it a rating on Amazon and/or GoodReads.

Want to learn more about the Magic Cube?
Check out my website:
www.mitchelmareee.com

Join the Watsons as they race to

find a cure for:

The Glitter Pox: book #4

Raina stood in front of the glass and flipped a switch. The glass lit up, and they could see into the crowded room beyond it. The room was lined with what looked like giant bird nests of straw, sticks, and cotton, each containing a sleeping dragon.

"Oh, my!" Violet gasped, her hand flying to her mouth.

"They look gross!" Parker blurted out, stepping back from the window.

Parker was right; the dragons didn't look good. Each was a different shade of purple or red. Bright pink sparkling spots covered every inch of their bodies from head to tail.

At first glance, it appeared the dragons were sleeping. Upon closer inspection, it became clear that their eyes were so swollen they could no longer open them. Their entire faces looked puffy and deformed.

The children looked from the sick dragons to Raina; the difference was startling. Like DJ, Raina had the same midnight blue scales dotted with golden specks. The sick dragons were bright and colorful, with no trace of blue on any of them.

Raina's snout was long, and her eyes were wide and bright. On the sick dragons, it was hard to tell where the snout was; their faces looked like giant bubbles covered in smaller bubbles.

"This is what Glitter Pox does to us," Raina said, her eyes dropping from the window. "If we don't find a cure, all these dragons will die."

Acknowledgments

Once again, thank you to my wonderful children. Your advice, storytelling, and fantastic imaginations help inspire every book I write.

Thank you to my nieces and nephews for allowing me to use several of your names in this story. Drew (Dreckson), Sydnie (Sidray), and Averly and Kinley (Averly). The rest of you will show up in upcoming books.

Thank you to Kevin and Wes; you make a great PR Team and are always encouraging and supportive.

Thank you to Ola Snimshchikova, my brilliant illustrator, for helping bring the story alive and for creating such a delicious-looking cover.

Thank you to Shannon Burns at Wildflower Books for all your edits and suggestions.

Thank you to my beta readers for the advice and sometimes difficult criticism I need to make each story great.

About the Author

Mitchel Maree grew up lost in imaginary worlds. Now, she takes those adventures and creates magical stories to share with children everywhere. Mitchel loves folklore and legends, especially from Ireland. She loves to weave mythical creatures into her stories.

Mitchel currently resides in Dublin, Ireland, with her family. She enjoys spending time outdoors, exploring new places, playing at the beach, and reading mystery novels.